two travelers

christopher manson

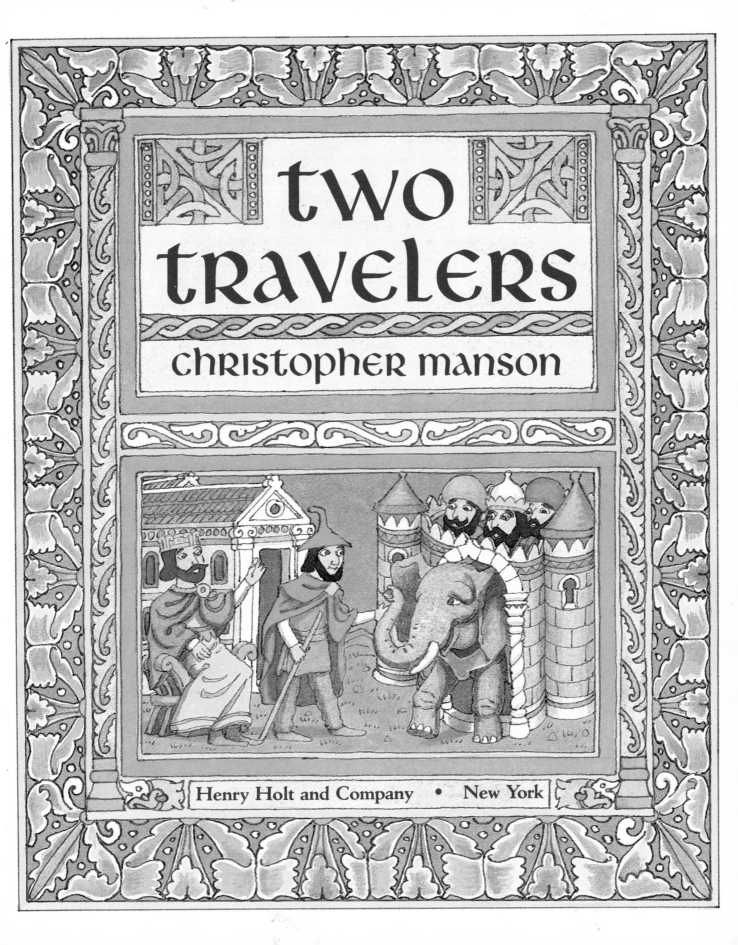

Henry Holt and Company • New York

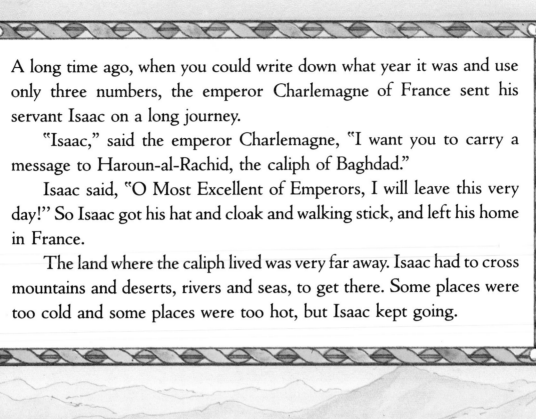

A long time ago, when you could write down what year it was and use only three numbers, the emperor Charlemagne of France sent his servant Isaac on a long journey.

"Isaac," said the emperor Charlemagne, "I want you to carry a message to Haroun-al-Rachid, the caliph of Baghdad."

Isaac said, "O Most Excellent of Emperors, I will leave this very day!" So Isaac got his hat and cloak and walking stick, and left his home in France.

The land where the caliph lived was very far away. Isaac had to cross mountains and deserts, rivers and seas, to get there. Some places were too cold and some places were too hot, but Isaac kept going.

When Isaac arrived in Baghdad, he went straight to the palace.

"O Great and Marvelous Caliph!" said Isaac, bowing low. "My master, Charlemagne, commands me to say that he wishes there to be peace always between his country and yours."

Haroun-al-Rachid said, "Tell your master, Charlemagne, that I, too, think there should be peace between us. And the best peace is that between friends. To ensure our friendship, therefore, I will send him a gift worthy of an emperor."

Haroun-al-Rachid clapped his hands.

The servants of the caliph appeared, leading an entire elephant!

"This," said Haroun-al-Rachid with pride, "is Abulabaz! He is my favorite elephant, so you must take very good care of him. Present him to your master, Charlemagne, with my compliments."

Abulabaz the elephant blinked his small eyes and rocked back and forth, and curled his long trunk around to sniff at Isaac.

"Thank you very much, I'm sure," said Isaac.

But Isaac wasn't sure at all.

Isaac had never in his life seen an elephant before and didn't know what to make of it. He saw a huge gray beast with two great flappy ears, two tails (one on each end), and two enormous white teeth that looked almost as long as Isaac was tall.

What will I do? thought Isaac. Truly, this Abulabaz is a monster! What if his huge round feet should happen to step on me, or his enormous white teeth should poke me, or he should want to eat me up for dinner! And how will I ever get this horrible ugly creature all the way back to my master in France? Oh my! Oh my!

And Abulabaz, for his part, didn't like Isaac either. He thought that Isaac had a strange smell, not like the people he was used to, and he wore a funny hat, besides. He wondered if Isaac was the kind of man who hit elephants with sticks or forgot to give them clean straw and water.

"Well," said Isaac, picking up his end of the rope, "it is going to be a very long trip back home. We'd best get started." And the two travelers left the hot, sunny land of the caliph.

For days and nights they traveled. When they reached a river, Isaac hired some river people to build them a raft of logs and sticks. Then he tried to coax Abulabaz onto it.

Abulabaz wasn't at all sure about the raft. He didn't think he liked rafts. But when he saw Isaac jumping up and down on it, he thought it might be safe. And when he saw that Isaac was not going to hit him with a stick, Abulabaz decided to give it a try.

So, very carefully, with Isaac holding his rope, Abulabaz stepped onto the wooden raft. He didn't jump up and down on it, like Isaac, but he did like the way it swayed gently under his feet.

The river people took their long poles and began to push the raft slowly up the river. It was hard work because elephants are very heavy.

Abulabaz rocked gently back and forth, enjoying the river breeze on his large, delicate ears, and he said, "Baroomph! Baroomph!" every time he saw a fish, which was pretty often.

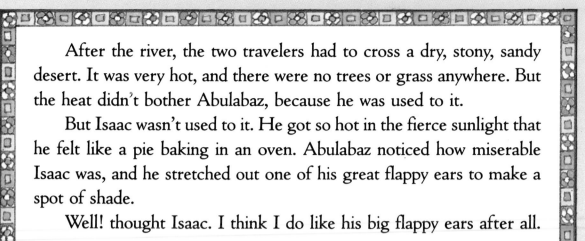

After the river, the two travelers had to cross a dry, stony, sandy desert. It was very hot, and there were no trees or grass anywhere. But the heat didn't bother Abulabaz, because he was used to it.

But Isaac wasn't used to it. He got so hot in the fierce sunlight that he felt like a pie baking in an oven. Abulabaz noticed how miserable Isaac was, and he stretched out one of his great flappy ears to make a spot of shade.

Well! thought Isaac. I think I do like his big flappy ears after all.

Soon the travelers arrived at a seaside town. All the little children followed them, clapping their hands and yelling and laughing. They knew elephants are just for fun.

Isaac felt foolish. "This is a most distinguished elephant!" he said as sternly as he could, but nobody paid him any attention.

But Abulabaz liked the children and felt very important. He said "Baroomph!" very loudly to make them laugh.

But when Abulabaz saw the sea for the first time, he didn't say anything. It wasn't like the river they had crossed. He couldn't see the other side of the water at all.

Isaac patted Abulabaz and said, "Do not worry, O enormous one! It is only the sea, and I shall take care of you."

Isaac bought two tickets on a stout little boat, and he made sure that Abulabaz had plenty of clean straw and fresh water. And they sailed away.

At first Abulabaz was scared of all that water, so Isaac held his trunk and told him that everything would be all right.

He showed Abulabaz how the billowing sail caught the wind, and how the large rudder steered them safely through the water. He even asked the sailors to sing some sailor songs, which they did gladly.

It didn't take long for Abulabaz to get used to the sea. Soon he was saying "Baroomph!" whenever he saw a fish (which was pretty often), so Isaac knew that he was all right.

But there was trouble ahead.

When their little boat was halfway across the sea, a terrible storm came up. And what a storm! The sky was black with rain, and the wind was so strong that the sail was ripped and torn. There were great peals of thunder, and lightning flashed across the sky. The little ship was tossed and turned so much that no one knew where they were headed—unless it was to the bottom of the sea!

All the sailors said their prayers, and Isaac shook with fear.

But Abulabaz thought the storm was wonderful! He liked rolling from side to side as giant waves tossed the ship. He thought the lightning was pretty. And the roaring thunder sounded just like a herd of elephants running. Abulabaz lifted his trunk and said "Baroomph! Baroomph!" at the sky.

Then a huge wave struck the boat, and Isaac was nearly thrown overboard, but Abulabaz caught him with his long, strong trunk. He kept it curled snugly around Isaac's chest, and Isaac felt safe.

Well! Isaac thought. It's very sensible indeed to have a tail stuck to the front end, too.

Finally the storm broke, the sun came out, the sea calmed. At last the travelers reached land again, and they walked through a second sea town. The people there had never seen an elephant before. They thought Abulabaz was a horrible monster!

Some of them rang bells and made noise, and some of them ran home and barred their doors and windows, and some of them simply stood and stared.

But the little children knew what to do. They all ran after Abulabaz, laughing and yelling, because they knew elephants were just for fun, even though they had never seen one before.

And Abulabaz felt very important.

"Our journey is nearly over," Isaac said to his companion as they started to climb into the high mountains beyond the sea. The mountains were wild and the trail was twisty, and there were only two or three narrow places where travelers could squeeze through.

When they were halfway across the mountains, it began to snow. Abulabaz had never seen even one snowflake before, much less a million snowflakes all at once. The poor elephant started to shiver and shake, and the snow piled up higher and higher. Abulabaz had never been so cold in all his life!

Isaac saw that Abulabaz's huge, delicate ears were turning blue, and he took off his own warm cloak and tied it around Abulabaz's head like a giant scarf. The cloak kept Abulabaz warm enough to go on. And his big, flat, round feet tramped down the snow and cleared a path for Isaac to follow in.

Well! thought Isaac. It's a good thing elephants come with great big feet after all.

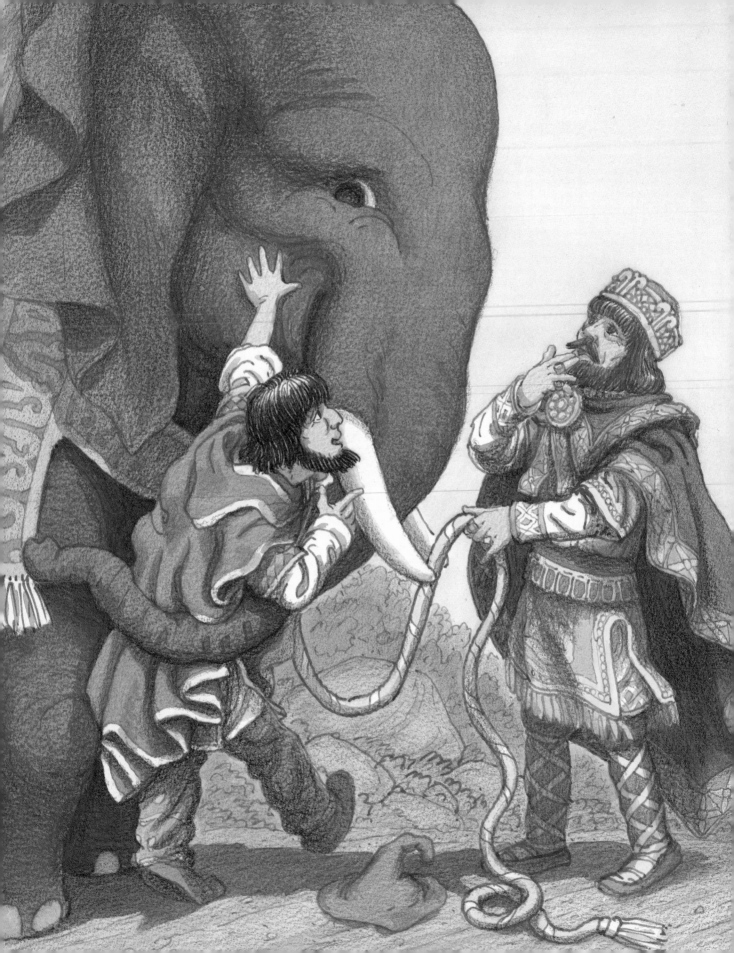

When the two travelers came down on the other side of the mountains, they were in the land of France at last.

Isaac led Abulabaz to the emperor Charlemagne. He said, "O Greatest of Emperors! I have taken your message to Haroun-al-Rachid, in far-off Baghdad. The caliph wishes to be your friend, and he sends you this gift worthy of an emperor." Isaac patted the elephant's side proudly. "His name, your highness, is Abulabaz."

"Ah!" exclaimed Charlemagne. "How wonderful! How unique! An Abulabaz just for me!" Then he leaned toward Isaac and asked in a low voice, "Tell me, Isaac. What does one do with an Abulabaz?"

"Why, your highness," said Isaac with surprise. "Why, O Greatest of Emperors, one does not *do* anything with him. One just . . . *has* him. He's a very wonderful thing to have."

"Ah! I see, I see," said Charlemagne, nodding his head wisely. But he was not sure that he did see.

Charlemagne gave Isaac a sack of golden coins for going all the way to Baghdad and coming all the way back again. Then he asked Isaac to take another message to another king in a far-off land. "You may go now," he said.

Isaac looked at Abulabaz. He reached behind Abulabaz's ear and scratched it in the way he knew Abulabaz liked. He said, "Thank you, my friend, for being such a good traveler. They will take good care of you here." Abulabaz took hold of Isaac's hand with his trunk one last time. He said, "Baroomph," very sadly.

Charlemagne had a splendid house built for Abulabaz in the palace gardens and made sure that he always had fresh straw and cool water. And when people came to visit, Charlemagne led them to Abulabaz and said proudly, "This is my Abulabaz! Is he not wonderful?"

And everyone agreed that he was wonderful.

But little by little, Abulabaz hid farther and farther away in a corner of the garden, until finally he wouldn't come out at all. He never said, "Baroomph!" anymore, not even when little children came to see him. He wouldn't eat his straw, and day by day he grew thinner and sadder. Charlemagne didn't know what to do.

News of Charlemagne's ailing Abulabaz spread, and soon it reached Isaac's ears in a faraway land. He hurried home to the emperor's palace and found Abulabaz in the corner of the garden.

"Oh my! Oh my!" exclaimed Isaac. He took hold of Abulabaz's trunk. "Abulabaz! What has happened to you, my once enormous friend? What has befallen you?"

Hearing Isaac's beloved voice, Abulabaz opened his small eyes. "Brump," he said weakly. He twined his trunk around Isaac's hand.

"Oh, Abulabaz!" Isaac said. "I have missed you so! I don't like traveling if you are not with me."

Abulabaz nodded his head to show that he understood.

"If I fetch you some sweet hay, will you eat it, my friend?" Isaac asked. Abulabaz said, "Brump." Isaac ran and brought the sweetest hay he could find, and Abulabaz took it from his hand and ate it. Isaac brought cool water, and Abulabaz sucked it up through his trunk and sprayed it into his mouth.

Isaac fed Abulabaz until he had eaten several bales of hay and could stand up by himself without looking so weak and wobbly.

Suddenly Charlemagne appeared in the garden. He saw Abulabaz looking happy and contented for the first time in months. When Isaac caught sight of his emperor, he feared that he would be sent away again, and he held tightly to Abulabaz. Charlemagne walked up to them and stroked his beard.

"I know why my Abulabaz was so sad," said Charlemagne, who really was a wise emperor. "He missed you, Isaac. It is clear that he needs you by his side to be happy. I command you to remain at my palace and be the keeper of my wonderful Abulabaz."

"O Wisest of Rulers!" Isaac said. "I gladly accept your command."

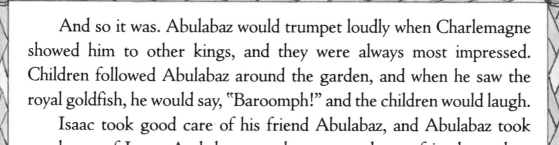

And so it was. Abulabaz would trumpet loudly when Charlemagne showed him to other kings, and they were always most impressed. Children followed Abulabaz around the garden, and when he saw the royal goldfish, he would say, "Baroomph!" and the children would laugh.

Isaac took good care of his friend Abulabaz, and Abulabaz took good care of Isaac. And they were happy as only two friends can be.

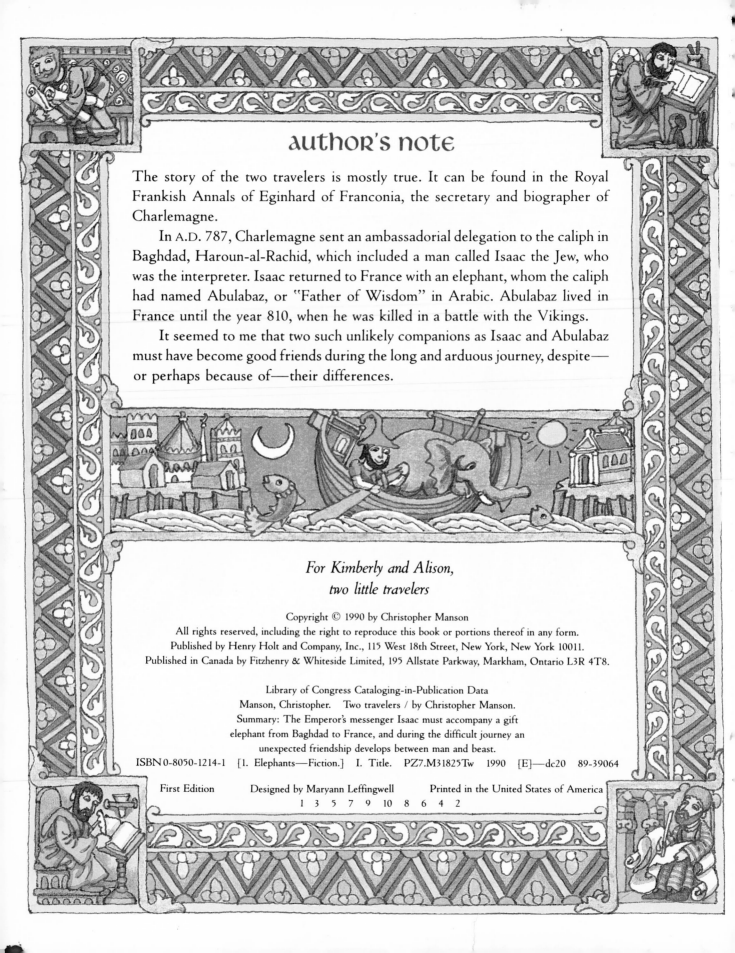

author's note

The story of the two travelers is mostly true. It can be found in the Royal Frankish Annals of Eginhard of Franconia, the secretary and biographer of Charlemagne.

In A.D. 787, Charlemagne sent an ambassadorial delegation to the caliph in Baghdad, Haroun-al-Rachid, which included a man called Isaac the Jew, who was the interpreter. Isaac returned to France with an elephant, whom the caliph had named Abulabaz, or "Father of Wisdom" in Arabic. Abulabaz lived in France until the year 810, when he was killed in a battle with the Vikings.

It seemed to me that two such unlikely companions as Isaac and Abulabaz must have become good friends during the long and arduous journey, despite— or perhaps because of—their differences.

For Kimberly and Alison,
two little travelers

Copyright © 1990 by Christopher Manson
All rights reserved, including the right to reproduce this book or portions thereof in any form.
Published by Henry Holt and Company, Inc., 115 West 18th Street, New York, New York 10011.
Published in Canada by Fitzhenry & Whiteside Limited, 195 Allstate Parkway, Markham, Ontario L3R 4T8.

Library of Congress Cataloging-in-Publication Data
Manson, Christopher.   Two travelers / by Christopher Manson.
Summary: The Emperor's messenger Isaac must accompany a gift
elephant from Baghdad to France, and during the difficult journey an
unexpected friendship develops between man and beast.
ISBN 0-8050-1214-1   [1. Elephants—Fiction.]   I. Title.   PZ7.M31825Tw   1990   [E]—dc20   89-39064

First Edition   Designed by Maryann Leffingwell   Printed in the United States of America
1   3   5   7   9   10   8   6   4   2